Tyler Is Shy

by Susan Hood
illustrated by Linda Clearwater

All-Star Readers™

Reader's Digest Children's Books™
Pleasantville, New York • Montréal, Québec

Ty liked shooting hoops.

He liked climbing trees.

He rode on his skateboard
as fast as a breeze.

But when other kids
came outside to play,

Tyler felt shy
and wandered away.

His mom said, "He's shy!
Oh, what can we do?"

His dad said, "Don't worry—
I was shy, too."

Still, Ty's mom suggested,
"Go outside and play."
"Not now, Mom, I'm busy,"
was all he would say.

One day a new kid
walked into Ty's class.

"Class, this is Susan,"
said Mrs. McFass.

The kids said, "Hello!"
but Sue looked away.

"She didn't say hi,"
Ty heard one kid say.

But Tyler had heard her!
She had said, "Oh, hi!"

She was just quiet
and Tyler knew why.

At recess the new girl
was still feeling shy.

Ty held out his yo-yo
and said, "Want to try?"

"You have a yo-yo?"
Sue asked. "I do, too!"
"I'm Tyler," said Ty.

The girl said, "I'm Sue."

Ty showed Sue some tricks that he'd learned to do.

Double
Loop-the-Loop

Home Run

Then Susan showed Tyler a new trick or two!

Texas
Cowboy

Walking
Two Dogs

The kids ran to watch.
They said, "Wow!"
They said, "Ooh!"

Ty grinned a big grin
and then—so did Sue.

They started a club
that day after school.
The kids all signed up.
They thought it was cool.

Now Tyler's still shy
and so's his pal Sue.

But that's fine with them—
and their new friends, too!

Words are fun!

Here are some simple activities you can do with a pencil, crayons, and a sheet of paper. You'll find the answers at the bottom of the page.

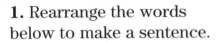

1. Rearrange the words below to make a sentence.

**kids   The   club   a
yo-yo   start**

2. Circle the two words in each line that rhyme.

try	**grin**	**why**
girl	**Sue**	**too**
school	**worry**	**cool**
hi	**shy**	**hoops**
new	**recess**	**to**
breeze	**play**	**away**

3. Do you remember your first day at school? Write a few sentences about how you felt.

4. How much of the story do you remember? Choose the word that correctly completes the sentence.

a. Tyler does tricks with a
yo-yo   ball   dog

b. Tyler rides on his
pony   skateboard   bike

c. The new girl in class is
loud   shy   busy

d. Tyler likes to climb
walls   mountains   trees

e. Tyler starts a club
**in gym   after school
at lunch**

f. Tyler makes friends with Sue
**in class   at home
at recess**

A Note to Parents

Read to your child...

★ Reading aloud is one of the best ways to develop your child's love of reading. Read together at least 20 minutes each day.

★ Laughter is contagious! Read with feeling. Show your child that reading is fun.

★ Take time to answer questions your child may have about the story. Linger over pages that interest your child.

...and your child will read to you.

★ Do not correct every word your child misreads. Instead, say, "Does that make sense? Let's try it again."

★ Praise your child as he progresses. Your encouraging words will build his confidence.

You can help your Level 2 reader.

★ Keep the reading experience interactive. Read part of a sentence, then ask your child to add the missing word.

★ Read the first part of a story. Then ask, "What's going to happen next?"

★ Give clues to new words. Say, "This word begins with *b* and ends in *ake*, like *rake, take, lake*."

★ Ask your child to retell the story using her own words.

★ Use the five Ws: WHO is the story about? WHAT happens? WHERE and WHEN does the story take place? WHY does it turn out the way it does?

Most of all, enjoy your reading time together!

**—Bernice Cullinan, Ph.D.,
Professor of Reading, New York University**

Reader's Digest Children's Books
Reader's Digest Road, Pleasantville, NY 10570-7000
Copyright © 2000 Reader's Digest Children's Publishing, Inc.
All rights reserved. Reader's Digest Children's Books and All-Star Readers are
trademarks and Reader's Digest is a registered trademark
of The Reader's Digest Association, Inc.
Fisher-Price trademarks are used under license from
Fisher-Price, Inc., a subsidiary of Mattel, Inc., East Aurora, NY 14052.
Printed in Hong Kong.
10 9 8 7 6 5 4 3

Library of Congress Cataloging-in-Publication Data

Hood, Susan, 1954-
    Tyler is shy / by Susan Hood ; illustrated by Linda Clearwater.
      p. cm. – (All-star readers. Level 2)
    Summary: A shy boy and a shy girl become friends and discover they
    share a common interest in yo-yos.
    ISBN 1-57584-657-8
    [1. Bashfulness—Fiction. 2. Friendship—Fiction. 3. Stories in rhyme.]
  I. Clearwater, Linda, ill. II. Title. III. Series.
  PZ8.3.H7577 Ty   2001   [E]—dc21   00-026300